IS IT HANUKKAH YET?

CHRIS BARASH

Pictures by
ALESSANDRA
PSACHAROPULO

ALBERT WHITMAN & COMPANY
CHICAGO, ILLINOIS

When frosty winds blow
and snow's all around

And there's no sign of green on
the trees or the ground...

Hanukkah is on its way.

When all forest creatures search for a den

Where they'll snuggle and sleep till spring blossoms again...

Hanukkah is on its way.

When we're all bundled up from our head to our toes

In layers and layers of warm winter clothes...

Hanukkah is on its way.

When glitter and paper are spread on the floors

And we hang decorations on windows and doors...

Hanukkah is on its way.

When cousins come over to stir, fry, and bake
The applesauce, latkes, and cookies we'll make...

Hanukkah is on its way.

When we count colored candles we'll use for the lights
To fill our menorah on eight special nights...

Hanukkah is on its way.

When the blessings are said and the first candles glow

And we're singing sweet holiday songs we all know...

When we're spinning our dreidels with family and friends

And hoping this wonderful time never ends...

Hanukkah is here!

Library of Congress Cataloging-in-Publication
data is on file with the publisher.

Text copyright © 2015 by Chris Barash
Pictures copyright © 2015 by Albert Whitman & Company
Pictures by Alessandra Psacharopulo
Published in 2015 by Albert Whitman & Company
ISBN 978-0-8075-3384-0

Printed in China
10 9 8 7 6 5 4 3 2 1 HH 20 19 18 17 16 15
Design by Jordan Kost

For more information about Albert Whitman & Company,
visit our web site at www.albertwhitman.com.

NOV 2 0 2015